The Snoring Log Mystery

The Snoring Log Mystery

Wilderness Adventures of a Young Naturalist

TODD LEE

The Snoring Log Mystery

Published by
Polestar Press Ltd.
6496 Youngs North Road
Winlaw, B.C., V0G 2J0
and
2758 Charles Street
Vancouver, B.C., V5K 3A7

Distributed in Canada by
Raincoast Book Distribution Ltd.
112 East Third Avenue
Vancouver, B.C., V5T 1C8

Published with the assistance of the Canada Council and
The British Columbia Cultural Services Branch.

Illustrations and cover design by Jim Brennan.
Interior design by Sandra Robinson.
Author photo by Jack Rushant
Printed and bound in Canada by Hignell Printers.

Canadian Cataloguing in Publication Data

Lee, Todd, 1924-

The snoring log mystery

ISBN 0-919591-76-0

1. Animals—Juvenile fiction. 2. Children's
stories, Canadian (English).* I. Title.
PS8573.E42S6 1993 jC813'.54 C93-091005-2
PZ10.3.L43Sn 1993

To my mother Shirley and my brother Eldon, who shared my wilderness world; and to my wife Holly, without whose encouragement this book would not have been written. *—Todd*

Contents

North To Canada

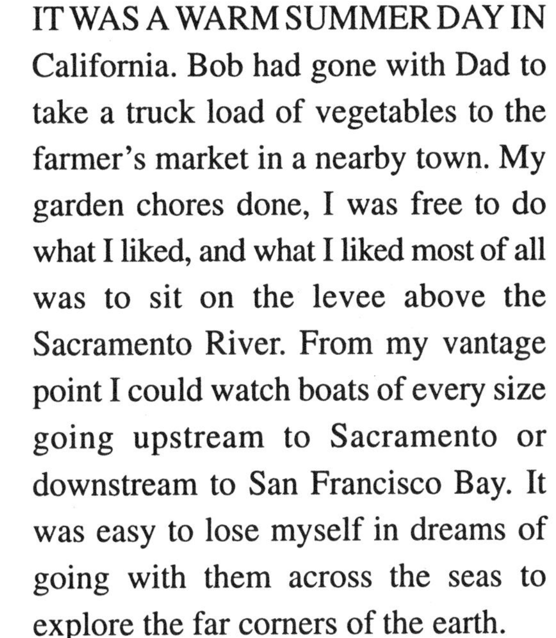

IT WAS A WARM SUMMER DAY IN California. Bob had gone with Dad to take a truck load of vegetables to the farmer's market in a nearby town. My garden chores done, I was free to do what I liked, and what I liked most of all was to sit on the levee above the Sacramento River. From my vantage point I could watch boats of every size going upstream to Sacramento or downstream to San Francisco Bay. It was easy to lose myself in dreams of going with them across the seas to explore the far corners of the earth.

I heard Dad's truck drive into the

farmyard, doors open and close, and then Bob calling my name.

"Gary! Hey Gary, where are you?"

"Over here—by the river," I shouted back. Bob knew where to find me. As soon as he came in sight I could see that he was really excited. Something big had happened.

"Gary, you'll never guess!"

"Come on, Bob, don't waste time. What's going on?"

"We're moving to Canada! There's a letter from Uncle Charlie. He wants Dad to manage a cattle ranch 'way off in the woods, and Dad is going to do it! Isn't that great news?" Bob stopped to catch his breath.

"But...but...*where* in Canada?" I knew that Canada was a big country, even bigger than California, much, much bigger.

"In British Columbia! Dad said the ranch is nearly four hundred miles north of the Canadian border!"

Bob grinned at me and I grinned back. *Big* news? This was *super colossal* news. Everything else dimmed in importance. I could hardly take it in.

"Wha...when are we going to move?" I stammered.

"Real soon! Come on, let's go find Dad and find out all we can!"

Mom and Dad were busy making plans when we dashed in the house, but Dad took time to answer our questions.

"Will it be *wild?*" I asked.

"You bet it will be wild," Dad said, and winked at Mom. "It's

over three hundred miles from the nearest city, and thirty miles from any stores."

"Will there be lots of wild animals?" It was Bob's turn.

"Sure. Uncle Charlie said in his letter that there are all kinds of wildlife—moose and deer and bears."

"Wow! Will there be *lions?*" I asked. I wasn't sure I wanted to be around lions.

"Not African lions," Dad laughed. "But there are probably cougars, that's a name for mountain lions."

"...and wild *Indians?*" Bob gasped.

"You've been reading too many Western stories," Mom put in. "Uncle Charlie says we will have Indian neighbours, and a good thing, too. They can teach us things we will need to know."

"How about cowboys?"

"Of course," Dad replied. "We will have cattle to look after. You boys will be cowboys yourselves before long. Think you can ride a horse?"

"I...I guess so." I had never been on a saddle horse. Would it be scary?

The next few weeks were filled with feverish activity. Dad and Uncle Wayne gave careful attention to the car and truck, tuning up the motors and mounting the best tires they could buy. Finally it was time to pack and load.

Bob and I helped wherever we could, and stayed out of the way when they loaded the larger furniture. It seemed to me that

they would never get everything on the truck, but Mom and Dad had planned well. It all fit.

Moving day came at last! Dad started the truck and gave a long blast on the horn. We followed in the car with Mom. Bob and I had just enough room to sit in the back seat, bags and cases all around us. We didn't mind. All that mattered to us was that we were heading north—north to Canada!

North we went—for two solid weeks. The open plains of Oregon gave way to the timbered mountains of Washington. Bob and I had never been even a hundred miles from home. This was exciting beyond our expectations.

At one of our camps, someone gave us two collie pups. Dad made them a kennel and found a place for it on the truck. Bob and I could hardly wait each day until it was time to camp so we could play with Duke and Chuck.

At the Canadian border, the Customs Officer walked around the truck. Finally he came to the pups.

"Fine collies you have there. It's too bad we can't let them come into Canada."

Bob and I gasped. Leave our pups here, in the hands of strangers? The very thought brought tears to our eyes!

"Of course," the Officer went on. "We might make an exception—just this once."

We gasped with relief. Then the Officer winked at Dad, and chuckled. He had been teasing us all along!

At the end of our second day in Canada, we camped near a small town nestled between sagebrush-covered hills. Bob and I, snug beneath our blankets, watched the stars twinkling in a big new sky and found it difficult to sleep. The night was filled with strange sounds that tripped the springs of our imagination and set us to excited whispering.

Suddenly a mournful howl echoed from the hills:

Ah...owooooooo.

We moved closer together and waited to see if the cry would be repeated, half-hoping that it would not. Then it came again, louder than before.

Yip! Yip! Yip! Ahoowooo!

Hearing our startled response, Dad came and explained that it was only a lonely coyote howling for a mate. We listened as the coyote's howl was answered by another across the valley, and then by several others. Finally we drifted off to sleep, the wild medley echoing into our dreams.

Early the next day we saw herds of white-faced cattle and knew we were in ranching country. Once, two Indian boys riding rangy horses came scrabbling down a steep slope to the side of the road. They waved their hats and whooped as we passed. Bob and I shouted back. Already we were thinking of the days ahead when we, like these boys, would ride the ranges of the North.

That night we turned from the highway onto a narrow track which led into a dark tunnel of trees. An hour later we came to

a weathered rail fence and a rickety pole gate. Headlights swung across a field of waving hay, and then we saw a two storey log house behind a row of aspen trees.

Bob and I were thrilled to our toes. Strangers in a strange land, we already felt the call of the wild beckoning us to explore its secrets. What adventures lay ahead we could only imagine. But adventure could wait. We had followed the long road north to Canada and had come to journey's end. This was our home!

Call From The Wild

"BOB, DO YOU KNOW WHERE you're going?" For some time now we had been walking along single file without seeing a familiar landmark.

"Now that you mention it, I'm not sure that I do," Bob replied sheepishly. "I thought we were headed south but we should have come out onto the road by now if we were going in the right direction."

Bob paused to inspect the bark of a fir tree. It was a trick we often used to find direction; usually moss grew only on the north side of the trunk. Unfortunately we were in a heavily wooded area where moss seemed to grow on all sides of the tree.

"I think home is that way," I suggested, pointing.

"But that's only a guess," Bob replied. "From the slope of the land I'd say you're at least a quarter of a circle turned around. I think we should cross this canyon and follow the contour of the land. It might lead us to a creek—and all the creeks in this area flow south."

It was dark and getting darker with the shortness of a late October day. To make matters worse, a thick overcast shut out the stars and an unseasonable flurry of snow added to our difficulties. The wind swirled about, blowing first from one point and then the other, giving us no clue to the way we should go.

We could not have been more than three miles from home, but because of the isolation of our ranch we could wander for miles if we headed in the wrong direction. I was becoming quite worried and I knew that Bob was anxious too.

Suddenly, above the moaning of the wind in the treetops I heard another sound. It seemed to be coming from the dark dome of the sky. I gripped Bob's arm and drew him to a stop.

"Listen!"

We stood close together in a swirling sea of snow and darkness and strained to identify the sound. Then it came again:

Alonk! Honk! Alaw-onk!

The musical calls, coming from many throats, were repeated

"It was exciting to know that a family of geese would be raised on our ranch."

again and again. Some were directly overhead, some from further away, and some just coming into hearing range. Now we could easily identify the call of the Canada Goose.

"Geese!" said Bob excitedly. "Hundreds of them! Do you know what?"

"Sure," I replied. "They're migrating, and a good thing, too—the lakes will be freezing over pretty soon."

"You're right. They're pulling out of the country. But it's *where* they are heading, not *why* that interests me. Geese go *south* in the winter! Remember?"

Now I understood what Bob was talking about. Of course. What luck for us! Although we could not see the geese in the darkness, we could hear them clearly as they crossed above us in their migratory flight, one flock after another. Following this feathered compass, we made our way south through the stormy night until we saw the lights of home.

Mighty wanderers are Canada geese. Their familiar *honk-alonk* can be heard from the Gulf of Mexico to the northern rim of Baffin Island. Walking one day through a ricefield in California, I flushed a hundred of the handsome birds. On another occasion I paddled a canoe along a back eddy of the Yukon River where it crosses the Arctic Circle and found a flock of Canada geese sunning themselves on a sandbar. In both cases they seemed very much at home.

In early spring, often before the snow has completely left the

North, the chief gander leads his flock in their annual trek from Mexico and the southern States to the Canadian Provinces and northern Territories. In late autumn, when the young have become strong enough flyers, he leads them south again to leave the frigid winter behind.

Although Canada geese are true migrators, they are not blind slaves to location. Many do not fly all the way to the Arctic in the spring, but stop off at likely breeding grounds along the way. In the same manner, not all will go to the southern States in the autumn, but will stay at more northern points if the food is good and the weather is not too severe.

One summer day Bob and I were exploring along the edge of a beaver pond. Duke, our collie, ranged ahead of us, letting his curious nose lead him here and there on the track of some of Nature's marsh inhabitants. While we stopped to pluck cattail canes to use as imaginary spears, Duke disappeared from sight into a clump of reeds.

Suddenly we heard a tremendous commotion, a great squawking and hissing, and Duke shot out of the grass with a pair of angry geese flapping in pursuit. They stopped a few yards short of us while Duke cowered behind our legs. Giving voice to threatening honks, the geese took to the air and circled over our heads.

"Say, I wonder if they are nesting?" Bob said. "Must be something like that to make them so angry."

Keeping a watchful eye on the circling geese, we moved forward until we could see beyond the clump of grass. Sure enough there was a nest, a mound of moss and feathers on top of a beaver lodge. We could make out the outline of four large eggs buried in goose down. Mindful of Dad's instructions to leave such nests alone, we quietly retreated and raced home to tell our parents. It was exciting to know that a family of geese would be raised on our ranch.

One of this pair of geese had an unusual pattern of white markings on its head and throat. Because of this we were able to discover that the pair came back to our ranch year after year. Although we did not always find their nest, we had the opportunity every summer to watch the young geese. They stayed at the same marshy pond until they were old enough to fly.

The young geese were dependent on the safety of the pond or the fierceness of their parents for protection until they were grown. Only then would their wing feathers be sufficiently developed to lift their large bodies into the air.

"Sometimes they rose into the air and flew aimlessly around the barnyard."

One summer a tragedy befell the goose family. When we rode by the beaver pond

we saw only two of the young geese. The parents were nowhere to be found. The remaining goslings seemed terrified when we approached and swam rapidly to the centre of the pond.

Bob and I were riding to the post office and had no time to look for the lost birds, but we were sure something had happened. The parent birds would never leave their young alone.

The following day we returned to the pond, hoping that the missing geese had returned. Again we found only the two we had seen the day before. We circled the area, looking for clues. On a marshy flat we found the answer—goose feathers scattered over a wide area. We had no doubt now. Something, probably coyotes, had attacked the geese. The brave parents had lost their lives defending their young.

Bob and I had a hurried discussion. How would the two young geese survive on their own? It seemed more likely that they, too, would fall victim to some predator, since they were unable to fly. We decided at last that we would try to catch them and raise them at home. It was easier said than done. The goslings were out in the middle of the pond where the water was over our heads.

"I know what we can do," Bob said finally. "We'll build a raft."

In short order we had dragged fallen pine poles to the water's edge and roped them together with our lariats. Soon we were poling our makeshift vessel out into the beaver pond. The

goslings honked in alarm and swam away, but there was nowhere to go. Then, to our surprise, they left the water and ran into the woods, using their wings to speed them along.

"All right," I shouted excitedly. "We can catch them now!"

We poled to shore as rapidly as we could, and ran after the fleeing geese. When we came upon them we discovered how easily they would have been caught should a coyote or fox have come along. Bob went after one while I closed in on the other. They flapped their wings and hissed, but moments later each of us held a goose in our arms.

Once caught, the goslings proved surprisingly tame. We must have presented an amusing sight when we walked into the ranch house, each with a long goose neck craning out of our arms.

"Hey Mom, just look what we've got! Can we keep them?" we shouted in unison.

"Wherever did you get those birds?" Mother asked. "Have you been bothering that goose family? Your father told you…"

"Oh no, we didn't take them away from their parents," we protested. When we told the story of the tragedy at the beaver pond, Mother said that we could try to look after the hefty youngsters.

Our task was not difficult. We found that the goslings would eat almost anything we gave them. Christened Willy and Nilly, they took up residence with our flock of chickens and soon had

the chicken yard completely in their control. If one of the hens were to get possession of a chunk of bread before the geese had their share, Willy and Nilly would go hissing after her. One gosling would seize the hen's neck in an ample bill while the other snatched the bread. Then they would squabble noisily over the spoils until it had all vanished down one of the long throats. Eventually the geese became so fierce with the hens it was necessary to banish them from the chicken yard. They then roamed at will about the ranch.

Whenever Bob and I came out of the house, the comical geese would come flapping and squawking to meet us, knowing that we usually carried a crust of bread or a handful of grain to reward them. Often they would follow us about, craning their necks around our ankles or gaggling together behind us.

September came with crisp frosty nights. Willy and Nilly had learned to fly. At first they went only a short distance, flying across the yard to meet us instead of running. As their wings became stronger, they grew more daring, rising to soar around the barnyard to the consternation of the chickens. No doubt the hens thought they were predator hawks. Occasionally Willy and Nilly were gone for hours, probably flying off to a nearby marsh to feed. Always they returned at night, for their attachment to us was strong.

September gave way to October. Flocks of crows and blackbirds gathered in the stubble and discussed travelling plans

in noisy committees. The day came when the first flock of wild geese flew over in a sharp wedge against the blue autumn sky.

Willy and Nilly were excited. They craned their long necks skyward and honked anxiously whenever a new flock went over. Sometimes they rose into the air and flew aimlessly around the barnyard.

One night a flock of geese spent the night in the stubble of our grainfield. We could hear them talking among themselves through the evening hours. In the morning they rose in a body, but instead of leaving they chose to circle over our barnyard. Willy and Nilly took to the air, honking frantically. The leader of the wild flock brought his crew around for one more circuit. There was an unmistakable invitation to his honking. Our two friends circled back over us, craning their heads down, honking—almost sadly, we thought. Then they rose higher, climbing swiftly after their wild cousins.

The call of the wild was powerful enough to overcome the bond between us and our feathered companions. Although we were sad to see them go, we were thankful for the time they had lived with us and for all the fun we had. With the wisdom granted by Nature, they would follow their migratory path south across the continent. We would not have willed it otherwise. Perhaps, someday, they would return to the place of their birth.

The Bravest And The Best

SHE HAD NO WARNING, NO TIME to hide. Like a thunderbolt the hawk plummeted from the sky, talons thrust forward to pierce tender flesh.

Caught in the open with her flock of fluffy chicks, the bantam hen shrieked a command that sent the chicks scattering while she dodged frantically to one side. The cruel talons missed their target but the hawk's braking wing struck the mother a blow that knocked her sprawling in the dust.

I ran to the rescue, shouting, knowing I would be too late. The chicken hawk spun around to claim his prey. A dozen orphan chicks would cry for their mother that night.

Suddenly a feathered bronze ball struck the hawk! Two pounds of fury, the banty rooster flew right into the face of the fierce enemy four times his own size. Feathers flew in clouds as the two unequal contenders tumbled in a whirlwind of dust.

There could only be one ending, I thought, the plucky rooster becoming the victim in place of the hen. How could he win against such odds? I was mistaken. Used to the role of attacker not attacked, and confused by the fury of the banty's onslaught, the hawk fell back.

At this point the rooster might have escaped, but he had no intention of running. Squawking angrily, he flew again at the hawk, sharp beak aiming for flashing eyes, ignoring the beating wings.

Sheer courage won the battle. With a scream of anger and disappointment the chicken thief launched into the air and flapped away into the trees.

The banty rooster remained on the battlefield. Only when he was sure that all was clear did he turn his attention to the hen who had risen weakly to her feet. While she called her chicks from their hiding places and hurried them to shelter in the chicken run, he stood alert guard, a small David ready to take on any Goliath.

One year a neighbour gave Bob and me a goat kid to raise. As 'Billy' grew, we had great times playing together. We thought he

"A rocky point jutted out from the shore and there, his back to the rock, stood a buck deer ..."

was tops, but we didn't know that our brave little pet would soon become a barnyard hero.

That there was only one goat on the ranch could have meant that Billy was doomed to a lonely life. This was not the way he chose, however; he followed along with the flock of sheep when they went to pasture. As it turned out, I had reason to be grateful for his presence.

One evening the flock was grazing near the timber on the far side of the meadow. A coyote slunk out of the woods, hungry for mutton and expecting no trouble in catching a sheep for his supper.

In panic the flock packed together. Too far away to be of help, I watched in horror as the coyote swept in for the kill. Then, from the far side of the flock, a small black warrior moved to place himself between the sheep and the attacker.

"Billy!" I gasped. "Oh no, you'll be killed!"

If Billy was afraid he didn't show it. Down went his head and the coyote was faced with hard little horns leading thirty pounds of angry goat in a furious charge. Surprised for the moment, the coyote paused, then leaped to get at Billy's flank. Billy was more nimble than he. Rearing on his heels he spun around in time to drive his horns into the coyote's shoulder.

Cautiously the coyote backed away, intending no doubt to attack the flock from a safer angle. Billy, however, gave him no rest but followed him step by step, ending with another sudden

rush. It was enough for the bewildered coyote. Never had he seen a sheep like this! Tail between his legs, he slunk back into the timber. Brave little Billy danced back to the flock, undisputed champion of the field.

Coots are small black waterfowl who love company. They can fly but seldom do, preferring to swim about near the shores of ponds and lakes in flocks often numbering several hundred members. One of their enemies is the fierce bald eagle. Eagles have a fondness for coots and are happy to have them for breakfast, lunch and dinner.

In our travels around the rangeland Bob and I often watched flocks of coots bobbing and diving for food, and we tried to mimic their chirping calls. One day we witnessed a remarkable feat of bravery. In a lake near the ranch buildings, a flock of coots made their home. High on a broken fir tree overlooking the lake, a pair of bald eagles had a nest. Not surprisingly, the eagles considered the coots a ready source of food. We arrived at the lake just as mother eagle soared from the nest,

"A single coot swam out of the flock towards the open lake, an irresistable target for the eagle."

intent on seizing a coot.

"Hey!" Bob exclaimed. "That eagle is going to attack the coots!"

"Look out, coots!" I shouted. "Enemy bomber at ten o'clock!"

Out of the sky the eagle plummeted, while the coots frantically closed ranks. At the very last moment they dived beneath the surface. The eagle flapped up into the air for another attack.

"Why doesn't that eagle pick on someone her own size?" Bob sputtered.

"I guess it's Nature's way," I replied. "Coots are part of the food chain. Look, there she goes again!"

At that moment a surprising thing happened. A single coot swam out of the flock towards the open lake, an irresistible target for the eagle. The eagle swerved in her attack to focus on the new target, her outstretched talons splashing into the water where seconds before the coot had submerged. Frustrated, the attacker rose, circled, and dived again as the brave little coot surfaced and sank.

Time and time again the cycle was repeated while we watched in suspense. Each time the coot surfaced farther from the flock. The eagle was getting angry. She dived from lower and lower altitude, once misjudging her height and splashing heavily into the water. Finally, tired and frustrated, she gave up the venture and flapped hungrily off to look for more cooperative prey.

The courageous little coot, who had risked her life to lead the eagle away, swam perkily back to her friends, obviously pleased

with herself. We clapped our hands to applaud her bravery. Did the flock have some way of showing its gratitude?

Another day Bob and I were riding Dick and Tony along a wintry road when a doe and two fawns dashed across in front of us. They were obviously tired for their sides heaved and their mouths gaped open.

"They've been running hard," Bob said. "I wonder what has been chasing them?"

The mystery was solved a minute later. Around the next bend of the road was a pond covered with ice. A rocky point jutted out from the shore and there, his back to the rock, stood a buck deer facing three attackers.

"Wolves!" I gasped. "Look, they're ganging up on that buck!"

"He must be trying to give the doe and fawns a head start!" shouted Bob.

Although the buck had a huge rack of antlers, he was having a hard time meeting the concerted rush of the three wolves who were attacking from both sides. At each charge, the buck reared up to strike with sharp hooves. Once he caught a wolf on his sharp antlers and pitched it yelping into the snow. We watched in fascination.

"Hey, it's not fair to have three against one!" I said angrily. "We've got to do something, Bob!"

"I don't know," Bob hesitated. "The wolves are probably hungry. That's the way it is in the wild!"

"But the buck is trying to save his family!" I protested. "He deserves to live!"

"I think you're right," Bob conceded. "Come on, let's help!"

Shouting at the top of our voices, we charged our horses around the edge of the lake. Caught by surprise, the wolves turned away from the deer to assess this new situation. It was more than they bargained for. Moments later they fled into the trees. The buck bounded off in the other direction, no doubt to rejoin the doe and fawns. This time again the hunted won and the hunters went hungry!

In the world of fur and feather, it is the bravest and best who survive. There are no awards for outstanding service. If there were, I would nominate a cocky banty rooster, a comical little goat, a perky water coot, and a noble buck deer, all of whom were ready to risk their lives to save the lives of others.

Eggs Are Where You Find Them

QUACK! QUACK! QUACK!

The wild mallard duck jumped from under my feet and so startled me I almost tumbled into the stream.

"Hey, Bob...!" I called, then gave a cry of dismay. A fierce hawk plummeted out of the sky and struck the climbing duck. There was an explosion of feathers and one anguished squawk, then silence. Horrified, I watched the hawk wing its way to a nearby tree, the forlorn body of the duck in its talons.

"Oh, how awful!" Bob bounded up and shared my dismay as we watched the hawk begin to feed on its prey.

"I didn't know a hawk would attack a full grown mallard!" I gasped. "That poor duck. She didn't have a chance!"

We had ridden our horses to our favourite fishing stream and were hiking to a beaver pond to try our luck when the mallard burst from the grass.

"I wonder what a duck was doing up here in the grass anyway?" Bob said finally. "Do you suppose it was on a nest?"

"Let's look around and see what we can find," I answered.

Carefully we searched through the heavy clumps of grass. There were many places where a duck could hide its nest, but after ten minutes we had found nothing.

"She could have moved away from the nest when she heard us coming," Bob suggested.

We widened the area of our search. A few minutes later I cried out. "Here it is, Bob! Just look at these eggs!"

There were five eggs clustered in the softest nest imaginable. It was lined with thick layers of down which the duck must have plucked from her own breast. Light turquoise in color, the eggs were half the size of a chicken egg. The nest itself was hidden in the center of a rank clump of grass and could not be seen from above.

"Say, I wonder if we could hatch these eggs under one of our hens?" Bob exclaimed. "We could have our own family of mallard ducks!"

"We were terribly anxious to see how big the egg of an eagle might be, but when we tried to climb the tree the parents screamed so fiercely we quickly gave up."

"They would get cold on the way home," I pointed out. "But if we could think of a way to keep them warm it would probably work. One of the hens has just begun to set; she wouldn't know the difference."

"Let's go home and see what we can come up with. I'll cover the eggs with my jacket to keep them warm until we get back."

A few hours later we were back at the duck nest with a bucket of wheat, preheated on the kitchen range. We were careful not to jar the bucket as we rode home. Soon the eggs were tucked safely under a brooding hen in a nest at the back of the chicken house. We watched anxiously to see if the hen would mind, but it was soon apparent that she accepted the eggs as her own. Now it was a waiting game.

It was three weeks before Bob and I learned the outcome of our experiment. One day we heard a chorus of *peeps* from under the hen. Bursting with excitement, we lifted the scolding hen to reveal five tiny down-covered ducklings!

Mother hen did her best to raise those strange members of her family, but they were a great trial to her. Whenever she took them to the creek for a drink, the ducklings would hop in and swim. The hen stalked up and down, clucking and scolding in a loud voice. Probably she was asking herself—"What will these modern children do next?"

One day Bob and I located the nest of a Great Horned owl in the

fork of a tree. While the mother owl swooped and hissed angrily, Bob climbed to the nest for a look. He found three brown spotted eggs slightly larger than those our hens laid.

"I wonder..." Bob looked down at me and grinned.

"No you don't!" I shot back. "We're not going to make a hen mother a clutch of baby owls! That would be cruel!"

There were many varieties of birds that spent the summers in the area around the ranch. Bob and I were always on the lookout for nests. Dad had cautioned us to respect the privacy of any nesting birds we found. Frequent inspection could lead enemies to disturb the parents or destroy the eggs.

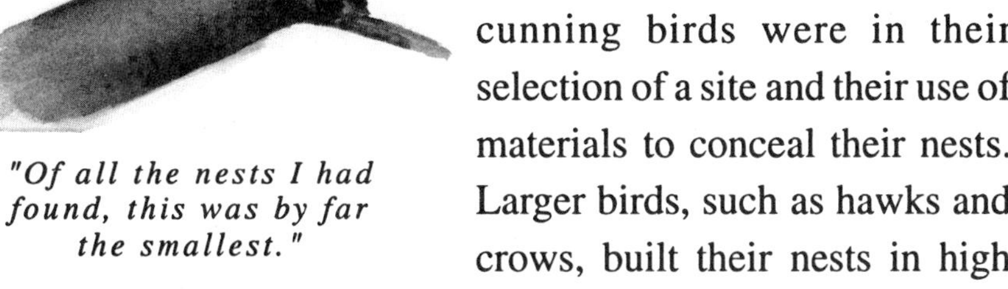

"Of all the nests I had found, this was by far the smallest."

We were amazed at how cunning birds were in their selection of a site and their use of materials to conceal their nests. Larger birds, such as hawks and crows, built their nests in high trees and were easily spotted, but smaller birds made every effort to hide their nests from enemies.

I was anxious to find a hummingbird nest. I watched a mother bird darting from bloom to bloom in Mother's flower bed and carefully noted the direction she took when she left. Each time

she disappeared in the branches of a spruce, but try as I might, I could not locate her nest.

As was often the case, I discovered the nest by accident. A lichen-covered knot of moss on a low spruce limb caught my attention one day. Drawing closer to inspect it, I became aware of two tiny eyes watching my every move. Moments later a hummingbird buzzed angrily away. I had found her nest!

Of all the nests I had found, this was by far the smallest. Less than two inches in diameter, the nest was built of bits of plants and grass, and lined with soft fibres from the catkins of cottonwood trees. The outside was covered with lichens from the spruce tree so that it blended perfectly with its natural surroundings. The nest contained four tiny white eggs, no larger than beans.

At the other extreme was the nest of the bald eagle. We found one on a high hill overlooking a lake. Fearing no enemies, the parent birds made no attempt to hide their nest. No crow or raven would try to steal their eggs! The structure was made of limbs piled one on the other until a platform nearly eight feet across was completed. We were terribly curious to see how big the egg of an eagle might be, but when we tried to climb the tree the parents screamed so fiercely we quickly gave up. We had to go to our encyclopedia to learn that an eagle's egg is over three inches long and two inches in diameter.

Easiest of nests to find were those of barn swallows. Every spring these restless birds returned to the ranch and built their nests of mud, glued to the rafters of the hay loft. Sometimes after a heavy rain some of these nests would break loose and drop to the soft hay below. Bob and I risked life and limb climbing up a shaky ladder to plop young birds into any nest we could reach. The hapless chicks seemed to be cared for by their new parents, or perhaps were still fed by those who had hatched them in the first place.

Sometimes we paddled our canoe along marshy shores, looking for the nests of water birds, or for those who preferred to be near the water. Grebes used lily pads to float their nests. Only hours after the chicks hatched, they found their way into the water and swam along behind the parent birds or rode on their backs.

Bob and I were delighted when we found the nest of a marsh wren. Of all the nests we had found, this was the coziest. Made of the soft down from cattail plumes, it was four inches high and completely enclosed. A tiny entrance hole let the mother bird come and go. When the wind blew, the nest became a tiny cradle which rocked the babies within.

While the nests of eagles were huge, elaborate structures, and those of the wren and hummingbird were soft and cozy, the nests of the killdeer and nighthawk were neither. In fact, they build no nest at all, but lay their eggs in a hollow depression on the ground. The colouring of their eggs blends so closely with the area around they are almost impossible to see. Bob found one such nest and called me to see it. Only when he pointed directly to the nest was I able to see it for myself.

One spring I took hammer and nails and built a bluebird house, a small structure with one entrance; I knew that bluebirds nest alone. Bob was equally busy building an apartment house for purple martins who like to have close neighbours. When we were finished, we anchored the bird houses securely in adjoining aspen trees. Would the birds take to the new lodgings? We would have to wait and see.

"Hey Gary!" Bob said excitedly one day. "The martins are here and looking at *my* house!"

The martins were, indeed, considering housing options. They looked at both houses carefully, then, to Bob's dismay, one pair chose my bluebird house for their home.

"But what will the bluebirds do?" I wondered.

We hadn't long to wait. A few days later we heard a terrible screeching and ran to the front yard. The bluebirds had arrived and were busy evicting the martins from *their* home. The disgruntled martins finally retired to the nest Bob had made, but they exchanged insults with the bluebird family for the rest of the nesting season.

Whenever Bob and I saw hummingbirds darting like bees from flower to flower, or great bald eagles soaring in lazy circles against the sky, we were thankful that we lived in the wilderness. Nature had a continuing store of surprises for us and every day brought discoveries that were new and exciting.

The Snoring Log Mystery

"HEY, HOLD UP A MINUTE, MY ski strap came untied!" Bob shouted.

Already over the crest and picking up speed, I hesitated to stop. "I'll wait for you at the bottom of the hill," I shouted back.

Leaning low over my skis for balance, I swept down the hill. It was exciting to have a free run after several miles of cross country skiing through heavy timber and windfalls.

Bob and I were *birch* hunting. In our part of the North there were ample stocks of spruce, fir and pine, but hardwoods were scarce. Dad had broken the tongue on the bob sleigh he used to haul hay, and needed a straight birch from which to hew another. Bob thought he knew where we could find one, so off we went on our skis over three feet of snow. Bob carried an axe to fall a birch when we found one.

At the bottom of the hill, I let the momentum of the flight carry me up on a mound of snow that outlined a large fallen tree. Beyond it I could see the white trunks and lacy branches of a birch grove. Bob was right. There were several trees straight enough to make a tongue for the sleigh.

While I waited for Bob to come with the axe, I drank in the quiet beauty of the wintry world. Snow covered the landscape like a thick fluffy quilt. Each stump had a giant marshmallow top and the snow, clinging to evergreen branches, reminded me of creamy white icing on a cake. There was not a sound of the modern world to hint that it had even been invented.

And then I heard it, a low rumble sound that sounded for all the world like a snore! It continued for a full minute while I looked all around me and I became more and more puzzled. Were my ears playing tricks on me? I shook the parka hood off my head and listened again. Yes, it was definitely a snore!

"What are you looking at?" Bob had whisked down the hill and pulled up beside the log on which I balanced.

"I'm not looking, I'm *listening*! Can you hear anything?"

Bob flipped back his hood but heard nothing. The snoring

*"...Mama Bear may come back any moment!
We sure don't want to be here then.
Mother bears have no sense of humour..."*

had stopped. "What was it you thought you heard?" He looked puzzled.

"I heard someone snoring," I replied.

"Snoring! Are you kidding?" He grinned at me in an impish way that put me on the defensive.

"Yes, snoring! Something was snoring around here, close. I know that sounds far out, but just the same I heard it."

"Maybe Rip Van Winkle is snoozing under this log," Bob teased. "Or maybe you scooped up too much wind in your ears coming down that..." His voice trailed off and a surprised look spread across his face. The snoring had started again!

"See!" I said pointedly. "Now who's got wind in his ears?"

"You're right, there is something snoring! Let's investigate." Bob moved forward a few feet, listened, then moved again.

I worked my way along the top of the log toward the crown of snow that covered the upraised roots. The snoring grew louder but still I could see nothing. Bob, too, was looking puzzled.

I reached the end of the log and looked over. At once I discovered two things: a strong, musty odour, and a small hole in the snow under the roots of the tree. Whoever was doing the snoring was down there, under the snow.

"Hey, look what I've found!" I called out.

Bob skied around the end of the tree and bent over to listen. He wrinkled his nose at the smell, then stood up with a grin. "Know what? We've found a bear den!"

"A bear?" I exclaimed. Then the light dawned. Of course! Bears sleep through the winter. This bear had dug its den in the natural depression beneath the uprooted tree. The snow had buried the area deep, but warmth from the sleeping animal had kept a small hole open. I suppose the warm weather in the past week had roused the bear from its deep sleep, at least enough for it to snore.

"What should we do?" I asked nervously.

"Nothing," Bob replied. "The bear is having a good sleep so why should we disturb it? But let's come back once in a while to see what's happening."

We had found old bear dens before, but never one that was occupied. This was something new and we were curious.

Several times during the winter we returned to the den to look and listen, but nothing had changed. April came and warm winds blew. Water ran and cut deep trenches through the ice and snow. Here and there patches of bare ground appeared. Spring!

Again Bob and I saddled Dick and Tony and rode off to check the bear den. We were surprised to find the den open and empty. Bear tracks led away into the woods. We were about to ride away when we heard a low whimper from the den. I urged Dick closer, then gave a shout of surprise.

"Hey Bob, just look at this!"

Bob coaxed Tony up beside my mount. At the back of the den was a black, furry animal about the size of a large cat. A bear cub!

The little fellow studied us with bright, curious eyes, then began to whimper again.

"Come on, let's get out of here!" Bob exclaimed suddenly.

"Huh? Why? It won't hurt us." I was fascinated by our find.

"Because Mama Bear may come back any moment! We sure don't want to be here then. Mother bears have no sense of humour," Bob explained. I got the point.

The next time we visited the den both mother and baby were gone.

"The cubs are born during the mother's winter sleep and by spring they are big enough to follow her into the forest."

From the time bears leave their dens in the spring they begin to prepare for their winter sleep. They will eat almost anything: fresh meat they are able to kill, carrion, grass and roots of almost every variety; berries and whatever larger fruit are available; spawning fish from the shallow streams; bees and honey when they can be found; grubs, beetles and ants. Especially ants! Ants appear to act as a tonic for their digestion. Between the time they emerge from their dens and the time they go to sleep at autumn's end, they may almost double their weight.

Bears are not sociable animals. Unlike coyotes and wolves, the male bear takes no interest in the cubs—in fact, if he gets a chance he is likely to kill them. Each bear has its own territory in the wild and will not share it with any other bear. Black bears do not go into dens together. The cubs are born during the mother's winter sleep and by spring they are big enough to follow her into the forest.

A year or two after our experience with the snoring bear, Bob and I located a bear den all ready for winter but not yet occupied. The bear had torn up dry grass from a wide area to line its sleeping quarters. Since the bear was not around, we took turns crawling into the den and were amazed at how skillfully it was lined. A six-inch-thick blanket of grass covered the entire den, and a large pile of loose grass was stored outside, no doubt to close the entrance after the bear had gone into its bedchamber for the long winter sleep.

We had other adventures with bears. Sometimes Duke took after them and ran them up trees. Of course, I'll always remember the time when it was me who was up a tree. That was a scary adventure!

If I hadn't received the Brownie camera from a California photographer who visited our ranch, I might not have been so daring—or foolish. I wanted to fill an album with wildlife pictures. I had pictures of the baby moose who came to live with us, and one of a cow moose I had surprised in a willow swamp. I wanted a close-up picture of a bear for my collection. Bob laughed when I told him, and Dad warned me not to meddle with bears. That only made me more anxious to reach my goal.

One afternoon I rode Dick out on the range, looking for a hawk nest Dad had discovered. I wanted a picture of the young in their nest. I didn't find the nest, but on the way home I spotted a mother bear and two half-grown cubs busy tearing open an anthill. Heart thumping with excitement, I studied the situation. The bear family was too far away to show up on a snapshot. And I was sure I couldn't get closer without sending them away in fright. Then a possible solution flashed into my mind: maybe I could get them to climb a tree!

I knew that I should ride away and not bother them. That's what Dad would have told me. "Especially stay clear of a bear with cubs!" he had warned.

It was Duke who made up my mind. When he spotted the

bears, he ran towards them, barking furiously. Mother bear took one startled look and fled with her cubs. Duke was right behind them and gaining fast. It was too much for me. Throwing caution to the wind, I urged Dick into a gallop and thundered after them, whooping as loud as I could. That I might run into danger never crossed my mind.

The chase ended suddenly. When the fleeing trio reached the shelter of the woods, one of the cubs shot up a large fir tree, claws tearing chunks from the rough bark. The other cub followed. Mother bear whirled and bristled at Duke, growling angrily before she, too, climbed the tree. Soon all three were clustered in branches about ten yards above the ground.

"Mother bear whirled and bristled at Duke, growling angrily before she, too, climbed the tree."

"Couldn't be better!" I exulted.

Busy getting my camera ready, I hadn't noticed what was happening in the tree. When I looked, I was dismayed to see that the bears had all but disappeared in higher branches.

"Hey!" I exclaimed. "Hold on a minute!" But the bears continued climbing

until all three were huddled in a crotch perhaps twenty-five yards from the ground, far too high to photograph.

Duke looked at me questioningly, then launched himself at the tree, tearing off bits of bark with his teeth.

"What do you want *me* to do?" I grumbled. "Climb up after them?" Duke looked as though he expected me to do just that!

Then a solution flashed into my mind. Near the tree that held the bears was another tree that towered just as high. If *I* climbed *that* tree I'd be able to snap an even better picture.

With the camera slung around my neck I started up the tree, making use of notches in the rough bark for hand and toe holds until I could reach branches. In a short time I sat on a large limb directly across from the bear family.

Trembling with excitement, I prepared to snap the picture. Bother! The shutter was stuck. I found a sliver of bark wedged under the trip lever.

By the time I freed the lever I heard clawing and scraping and looked across to see mother bear's furry black coat disappearing down the trunk of her tree. The cubs didn't follow her but they moved around until the tree all but hid them from my sight.

What now? While I fumed with indecision, Duke's wild barking told me that the bear had reached the ground. Hey—maybe Duke would run her up the tree again. Suddenly I had a horrible thought: *what if Duke chased the bear up my tree?*

For a moment I was almost dizzy with terror. I looked down

"From the time bears leave their dens in the spring they begin to prepare for their winter sleep. They will eat almost anything..."

the tree—but I couldn't go down, the bear was there! I looked up—but mother bear could climb as high as I could!

Across the space in the other tree I saw the cubs peeking around the tree. They were trembling and whimpering. Why, they were just as frightened as I! In that moment I felt ashamed of what I had done—terrorizing the bear family just for a picture, forgetting Dad's warning. How foolish I had been! I gripped the branch hard and waited while waves of fear swept over me.

I guess Someone must keep special watch over foolish boys. A few moments later I saw the mother bear dashing away through the woods with Duke in pursuit. No doubt she was leading him away from her cubs, hoping that I would follow. Well, if that was what she wanted, I was glad to oblige! I fairly flung myself down the tree, sliding the last few yards to land in a heap on the ground.

Dick was gone! I suppose when he saw mother bear and Duke chasing each other around the tree he decided enough was enough. He and Duke would be waiting for me at the barnyard gate.

"So long, fellows—I'm sorry!" I shouted up at the cubs, then I took off in a direction opposite to that taken by the bear. Never again would Dad have to tell me—*Don't meddle with bears!*

Mystery Trails

"HEY BOB, COME LOOK AT THIS!"

Bob set down the bucket into which he had been plunking clusters of ripe blueberries and hurried over to join me. I was kneeling in the grass and looking intently at the ground. I could hardly wait to share my discovery.

"What have you got there?" Bob asked, dropping down beside me.

"See, it's a trail!" I said excitedly. "And a well-travelled one, too! What do you suppose could have made it?"

Bob parted the grass and saw a narrow trail, obviously worn down by the passage of many feet. But what tiny

feet they must be! The trail was no more than an inch wide and half that deep. Every piece of grass or twig had been removed.

"Perhaps it's a mouse trail," Bob guessed. "There must be plenty of mice around here."

"You may be right," I agreed. "But look here, the trail goes right under that branch. A mouse would have gone over it."

"Well, it must *go* somewhere," Bob answered. "Let's follow it and see what we can find. If mice made it we should find a nest or a hole."

Following the trail was slow work—it wound through deep grass, shrubs and clusters of kinnikinnick. It skirted a boulder and shied away from the overflow trickle of a small spring.

"Whoever they are they don't want to get their feet wet!" I chuckled.

Thirty feet away the trail came to an end in a mound of sand two feet high and three feet in diameter. At first glance it appeared that the entire surface was moving. On closer inspection, we found it was covered with thousands of tiny red ants.

"An anthill!" Bob exclaimed. "That trail was made by ants!"

"I don't believe it! How could anything that small make such a deep trail?"

Yet it was true. Although the trail we had observed seemed not to be in use, a similar track coming from the opposite direction carried a steady flow of tiny workers going out and coming in. Many of the incoming ants carried bits of food,

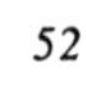

"It was amazing to think that these tiny creatures could wear a path into the ground!"

sometimes almost as big as the workers themselves.

The anthill was a large one and, by its appearance, quite old. It was amazing to think that these tiny creatures could wear a path into the ground! How many trips by how many busy worker ants over how many years did it take to do it?

Reading trails was something Bob and I could practice all year round. Sometimes Dad helped identify mystery tracks; sometimes Old Annie, our Indian neighbour, would share her wisdom with us; sometimes we puzzled things out on our own, as we did with the ant freeway.

When winter came, snow covered the ground for months at a time. Each new fall of snow gave new opportunities to practice our tracking skills.

Bob and I were aware that nature was not always kind and gentle. Some wild birds and animals were hunters; others were the hunted.

One day we were following the tracks of a snowshoe rabbit across the snow, trying to find out what it ate in the winter. It kept to the cover of the bushes, we noted, and made long hops when it was in the open.

Rabbits, like mice, are a danger to nothing, but they have many enemies. The bunny Bob and I followed chose to cross a frozen stream bed. That mistake was its last. Halfway across the open space the trail ended abruptly. The tragic story was imprinted on the snow in the form of wingtip marks and a spattering of blood stains. A great horned owl had swooped down on silent wings and carried the rabbit away for its supper.

Once we had the experience of being the tracked rather than the tracker. It happened in midwinter. A warm chinook wind had softened the snow, but then the weather turned cold. The result was a crust of snow that was heavy enough to bear our weight on snowshoes. Bob and I were exploring, searching for trees that would make firewood. Bob stopped suddenly and held up his hand.

"What's that?"

I looked over his shoulder and listened. For a moment it sounded like something heavy was breaking the crust. Then all was quiet.

"Did you hear something?" Bob's face looked strained.

"I...I thought so...but I don't hear anything now."

We moved on a short distance then stopped again. There was no doubt about it—something was following us! Was it a timber wolf? A prowling cougar? A bear that had left its den? The forest was tense with mystery. And fear!

"Bob...should...should we climb a tree?" I stuttered nervously.

Bob shook his head. "It's probably nothing to worry about. Let's just circle back towards the ranch—and keep our eyes open!"

We angled along a south slope where the sun had a chance to soften the snow. For the first time we could move without making a noise.

"Say, Gary," Bob said in a low voice. "Let's hide behind these bushes and try to see what's following us."

I nodded. We crouched down and waited. Moments later we heard steady footsteps, the snap of a branch, then we caught a glimpse of something grey. Bears and cougars weren't grey, but timber wolves were! We stiffened, ready to drop our snowshoes and dash for a tree. Then out of the bushes stepped a deer with a half-grown fawn.

My breath went out in a gasp of relief. Bob chuckled. The doe threw up her head and snorted, then she was gone, bounding into the thickets with her fawn at her heels.

"Then out of the bushes stepped a deer with a half-grown fawn."

Why had the doe been following us? Back at the ranch Dad came up with a possible explanation. Just as we were curious about the tracks of others in the woods, the deer was curious about us. She had meant no harm.

One summer day we were riding along a woodland path when we saw the fresh tracks of a horse going in our direction. We knew from the prints of the steel shoes that the horse was from one of the ranches, and not a wild mustang. A short time later the trail led through a dusty area and we could see a continuous groove paralleling the tracks.

"You know what?" Bob said. "I think that horse is dragging a halter rope. It must hold its head off to one side so it won't step on the rope."

"I wonder if it got away from someone? Maybe the rider is walking home."

We knew what that was like. Once a moose had run through the thicket where we had tied our mounts. Frightened, the horses had broken loose and trotted home, leaving us to follow on foot. That was no fun!

"Do you think we should follow it?" Bob asked.

"I dunno...it's not one of our horses. We should be heading home."

"I guess you're right. Still..." Bob looked again at the tracks. "Someone might be looking for this horse and not know where it went. Look, you can head home, I'll follow this up for awhile."

"Oh well, we can spare some time, I guess. I'll go with you," I said without enthusiasm.

At first the tracks were easy to follow, but then they crossed harder ground. The trail branched several times. Finally we

could find no prints at all.

"Some trackers we are!" Bob snorted. "Can't even follow a shod horse!"

"Oh well, we tried. We'd better tell Dad. Maybe he can find out who lost a horse." I was ready to ride back home.

Suddenly Bob's horse, Tony, threw up his head and whinnied. Almost immediately there came an answering *neigh* from a wooded draw below.

"Hey, that sounds promising. Let's go!" Bob swung back into the saddle. Our horses had scented the other and needed no guiding to search it out.

"There it is!" I called out.

As we had guessed, the mystery horse, a sorrel mare, was riderless. She carried no saddle, but wore a halter from which trailed a frayed length of rope. We saw at once that a knot in the rope was snagged on a log. In trying to break loose the mare had circled a tree and was hopelessly entangled.

"Wow! Just look at that!" Bob exclaimed. "She would never have worked herself loose. She would have starved to death if we hadn't found her!"

"And remember?" I shook my head. "We wouldn't have followed her trail if you hadn't insisted. Guess this was her lucky day!"

The Right Foot For Survival

"YOU GO AROUND TO THE OTHER side of the point and hide in the willows, Gary. I'll sneak along the tree line and chase him out to you. You're sure to get a good picture."

"How can you be sure he won't take off across the swamp?" I whispered back.

"The ground is too soft. Look, it's just a bog. It wouldn't even support one of us. We would sink out of sight."

"All right, but if it's that soft, be careful where you step. I'll whistle like a blackbird to signal when I'm ready."

The object of our excited planning was a huge bull moose feeding on a point of land that jutted into the lake. Upwind from us, he had not yet discovered that we were there.

I already had a picture of a cow moose, but I was anxious to have one of an antlered bull to add to my collection of wildlife photos. Finding a bull who was not aware of our presence seemed like a great opportunity. Between the moose and the lake was a swampy area—matted roots and grass saturated with water. Bob was sure the moose would shy away from this and run for the woods. This would bring him close to the spot where I would be hiding with the camera.

Bob waited until he heard my whistle indicating that I was in position. He began his stealthy circuit of the moose. When he judged that he was close enough to shy the moose in the right direction, he stood up and waved his arms. The moose flung up his head, testing the wind, then took off at a fast trot. To my dismay, he ran straight across the swamp, nowhere near my hiding place.

I watched in suspense, expecting sharp hooves to plunge through the surface of the bog. I was mistaken. The moose navigated the swamp safely, plunged into the lake, and swam to the other side.

"How did he do that?" I asked Dad that evening, after we had related our experience with the moose.

"Moose have the right type of feet for soft ground," Dad explained. "That long, pointed hoof is designed for walking on

"Say, that bird can come down the trunk head first!"

a hard surface, but when they are on soft ground, like yours was today, their toes spread far apart. A tough membrane between the toes almost doubles the size of their feet and makes it possible for them to walk where one would expect them to sink right through."

"Hey, that shows clever designing!" Bob said appreciatively.

Growing up on a wilderness cattle ranch gave Bob and me opportunity to discover many interesting things in the world of Nature. By close observation of our woodland neighbours, we learned that moose are not the only ones who have feet designed for survival.

Around our ranch we observed many varieties of the hawk family. They ranged in size from the robin-like sparrow hawk to the huge bald eagle with a wingspread of over six feet. In between were chicken hawks, duck hawks, red-tailed hawks, fish hawks, or osprey, and several types of falcon. All of them took their prey in the same manner, diving from the air to strike, then flapping away to a private limb to eat what they caught. The ranch lost many chickens, several cats, and even a baby lamb to raiding hawks. When Dad brought down a chicken thief with his shotgun, we were able to have a close look.

"See those feet?" Dad said. "Those long talons are as sharp as needles. Most birds use their talons to grip a perch, but hawks use theirs to kill. Once they pierce the flesh of a victim, the talons

contract and lock. No matter how hard the victim struggles, it can't escape."

"It must be awful for their victims," I remarked, gingerly testing the sharpness of the talons. "Hawks are cruel birds."

"It's part of Nature's balance," Dad explained. "Without hawks and other meat-eating birds and animals, mice and rats and rabbits would overrun the country. And it isn't as cruel as it might seem. Because a hawk's talons are so long and sharp, they usually strike a vital organ and kill their prey immediately. They have the right equipment for their role, but I sure wish they would take our chickens off their menu!"

Bob and I learned that some birds, like magpies and crows, spend much of their time on the ground. Their feet have short claws and sturdy toes that open flat and make it easier for them to walk. Woodpeckers, on the other hand, find their food under the bark of trees. Their feet have short toes, each capped by a sharp curving claw that penetrates wood fibres and makes it possible for them to hang on to a tree trunk.

One day we discovered a small bird we had not seen before. It was on the trunk of a tree like a woodpecker, but its activity was quite different.

"Say, that bird can come down the trunk head first!" I pointed out.

"How does it keep from turning a somersault?" Bob wondered.

"I don't know, but let's ask Dad."

As it turned out, Dad didn't know either. The next time he went to town, he brought us an illustrated bird watchers' handbook. It proved to be a storehouse of information.

"Here's the bird we were watching," I said excitedly. "It's a *nuthatch*."

"Does it tell how they can walk down a tree trunk?" Bob asked, peering over my shoulder.

"Uh-huh. They have a fourth claw that reaches back and hooks into the bark like an anchor when they go downward. That way they can find seeds and insects that other birds miss. I guess nuthatches also have the right feet for survival."

That first year when winter settled in with deep snow and frigid temperatures, we were curious to know how birds and animals would cope with such a major change. Some, we learned, like ducks and geese, simply flew south for the winter. Others, like bears and woodchucks, who weren't travellers, dug dens and slept until spring came again. Those who opted to tough it out were well-adapted to the change in climate.

Bob and I learned to use snowshoes when snow was too deep for walking. We were surprised to discover that some of our woodland friends did the same thing—only they *grew* their snowshoes. It was fascinating to observe how Nature equipped them so they could survive under the most adverse winter conditions. Bob and I often referred to our wildlife books to

explain riddles posed by tracks in the snow.

Lynx grow thick fur between their toes and around their feet, almost doubling their size—truly effective snowshoes. Not only does this make it possible for them to travel in soft snow, it also muffles the sound of their footsteps so they can stalk their prey.

Snowshoe rabbits adapt equally well to winter conditions. Not only does their fur turn from brown to snow-white, they, too, as their name implies, grow 'snowshoes' on their feet. Since rabbits are always the hunted instead of the hunter, this extra equipment gives them a chance to survive even when pursued by a hungry lynx.

The birds who stay for winter prepare by growing, under

"Snowshoe rabbits adapt equally well to winter conditions."

each feather, a downy second feather to double the warmth of their winter coats. Grouse, who forage on the ground for food, grow a webbing of hair along each toe so they can walk in the snow without sinking.

"Isn't Nature wonderful?" I said to Bob one day. "We have to buy heavy clothes and boots and snowshoes so we can cope with the change of seasons, but birds and animals just grow what they need to survive!"

A Moose In The House

"GET THAT MOOSE OUT OF THE house this instant!"

"But Mom!" I protested. "He's afraid of the thunder. He won't hurt anything!"

"I don't care—enough is enough! I'm not having a moose in my kitchen. Out!" Mother pointed resolutely to the door.

"Oh, all right, but it's a mean thing to do. Look how he's trembling!"

With the first clap of thunder Flip had begun to race around the house bleating with terror. Perhaps it reminded him of the crack of the rifle that had taken the life of his mother. On his third circuit of the building, I had opened the kitchen door and Flip darted for the opening. Sharp little hooves slid on the linoleum and the baby moose ended up in a heap behind the table where he lay, rain water dripping from his sleek brown coat.

"Well...he can stay on the porch if that would make you feel better," Mother said, relenting slightly.

Poor Mother! She had long since ceased to be amazed at the things Bob and I carried home to our wilderness ranch, but our latest find was a bit much to take. Well, what would your mother say if *you* brought home a moose and asked if you could keep it? But our mother was a good sport and when we told her the story of how we had found him she allowed the moose to stay. Flip (as we named our new friend, because his long ears flipped constantly) was soon very much at home.

Of course, Dad had warned us to leave the young wild animals alone if we should find them. Deer and moose especially are in the habit of hiding their young while they go off to feed. In this case it was different. We had found the body of a cow moose that some callous hunter had shot. Flip was nearby, bleating sadly with loneliness and hunger. When we brought a bottle and nipple (borrowed from our orphan lamb) and filled the moose calf's stomach with warm milk, he was so grateful he followed us home. Surely he was the most unusual animal we had living at our ranch.

"Someone must have ordered the wrong size of legs!"

"Just look at those legs!" Bob exclaimed. "He can't even reach the ground!" It was true. Flip had to kneel down to nibble shoots of new spring grass.

"Someone must have ordered the wrong size of legs!" I quipped.

"You can say that for his ears, too," Bob chuckled. "And whatever does he need a nose like *that* for?"

"How would you boys like to have someone talk about *you* that way?" Mother put in. "Those long legs will help him travel through deep snow or wade through deep mud when he grows up. And big ears will help him hear every little sound for his protection in the wild." But she, too, smiled at the ungainly appearance of our newest animal companion.

Bull moose are majestic and powerful. Largest of North America's wild land animals, they may stand as tall as a horse at the shoulders, weigh as much as 1800 pounds and carry antlers to the width of five or six feet. As large as they are, however, they are agile and graceful. I have watched a bull moose trot through lodgepole pines so thick it was difficult for me to force my way through with a horse; yet the moose made scarcely a sound. On another occasion Bob and I tried to overtake a moose with a canoe as it swam a lake but we were quickly outdistanced.

A baby moose, however, is only a promise of the noble creature it will become. Its legs are ridiculously long for the size of its body. Often when Flip turned suddenly, his legs became

tangled and he would fall in a heap. His high shoulders and short neck made it impossible for him to reach the ground, but this was not as much a handicap as one might think. Moose seldom eat grass but are more inclined to browse off the tender buds of trees and bushes. Their next favourite food is water lily root and for this they wade out to shoulder depth in lakes and ponds.

"How can we keep the dogs from bothering Flip?" was one of our first concerns when we learned that we could keep him. Flip solved this problem himself. When his stomach was filled with warm milk he looked for a place to rest. The shadiest spot was already occupied by our two dogs, Duke and Chuck. Undismayed, Flip folded up his long legs and settled down between them where he proceeded to nibble their silky ears in turn. The pups loved it and the three were soon fast friends who went everywhere together.

"We'll have to make sure he doesn't get into the barnyard," I suggested. No telling what reception he would get from the other stock. We worried especially about the stallion and the ram, and about milk cows with their long sharp horns.

Our anxiety was unfounded. One day the yard gate was left open by mistake and Flip wandered through. The great black stallion, Caesar, was first to see him. He threw up his head and snorted shrilly, then he rounded up his mares and herded them to the far end of the pasture. The ram was just as cautious; with his ewes he retreated across the barnlot and stood stamping the

ground nervously. The milk cows bawled loudly and ran to stand next to the pen where their calves were kept. I suppose they associated Flip's smell with that of a full-grown moose. Whatever the reason, Flip was undisputed master of the barnyard whenever he chose to stroll there.

Flip's devotion to his human companions was intense. While we were doing our correspondence school lessons he would lie next to the door with the pups, waiting for us to come out for recess or noon hour. When we appeared, he would bound to his feet and race to meet us, bleating his pleasure. He loved to have his silky ears and velvety nose stroked and when we scratched his back and stomach he would wriggle all over with delight. If we went through a gate and locked him behind he would race up and down and cry in distress. We seldom had the heart to leave him for very long.

By the time Flip was three months old all his clumsiness was gone. Fences were no longer a barrier to him; he would simply walk up and bound over them. With this new agility came a problem. Flip developed a fondness

"Bull moose are magestic and powerful ... as large as they are, however, they are agile and graceful."

for vegetables and found the garden fence one that he could easily leap. Mother was indignant when she found heads of lettuce and cabbage disappearing in wholesale quantities and rows of climbing peas and beans trampled down. Bob and I spent long hours stringing strands of barbed wire above the regular fence to curb Flip's forays in the garden.

Flip soon took to following us even when we were on horseback. While we could sometimes outrun him in the open, we were no match for his agility in the woods. Strangers seeing us go by must have rubbed their eyes in disbelief at what they saw. First came Bob and I loping on our ponies and giving loud whoops. Beside us Duke and Chuck raced, barking and yelping their pleasure at the outing; and behind came Flip, ears back, long legs carrying him in bounds that easily cleared logs and windfalls, all the time bleating at the top of his voice to add to the din!

Flip's fondness for water was almost as great as our own. After a hot day working in the hayfield or pitching hay back in the loft of the barn, Bob and I would saddle our ponies and ride three miles to the stream where a beaver pond made an ideal place in which to cool off. When we arrived it was a race to see who could strip off his clothes first and dive into the cool waters of the pool. Meanwhile Flip would wade in to the water to shoulder depth and happily bob for tasty bites of marsh grass and lily roots. When he swam he kept his head and neck high and

seemed to be almost leaping through the water, faster than either Bob or me, even faster than the pups who could swim circles around us. By the time we had dried ourselves off ready to slip back into our clothes, Flip would join us and shake so vigorously we would have to dry all over again!

Flip would eat almost anything: grass and roots, buds and tender twigs from bushes, vegetables from the garden, scraps and crusts from our sandwiches, even wild cucumbers and hop vines that ran up the side of our house. I think he took a mischievous pleasure in approaching the horses when they were given their mid-day treat of a bucket of grain. He seemed to know that they would shy away and leave the grain to him. We always took pity on the horses, however, and lured Flip away with a lump of sugar. Flip had a well-developed sweet tooth.

Like most of the wild animals we brought home, Flip returned to the wild when he was grown. We hoped with all our hearts that he would be able to survive and be contented among his own kind. From the months we spent with him, however, we learned much about another of the wonders of Nature, and this chapter in our lives left fond boyhood memories.

Forest Pincushion

ARF! ARF! YIP!

Frenzied barking erupted from a thicket near the trail Bob and I were following to a blueberry swamp.

"Here Duke. Here Duke!" I called. Only moments before the collie had darted into the bushes.

Arf! Yip! Yip! was the only response.

"We'd better have a look," Bob suggested.

As we turned from the trail there was a sudden change in the uproar Duke was making.

Ai-eee! Ai-eee! Ai-eee! Excited barking changed to howls of pain. Duke shot out of the bushes, whining frantically and pawing at his face.

"Hey, he's chuck-full of quills!" Bob shouted, pointing at Duke's face. "The mutt must have been after a porcupine!"

"Stupid dog!" I scolded. "Don't you know better than to fool around with a porcupine?" Duke whined and dripped his tail between his legs. I think he knew that he should have had more sense.

"We've got to get them out right away," Bob went on. "You want to hold him or pull quills?"

"I'll hold him!" I replied quickly. Bob was always prepared to care for our animals when they were hurt or sick.

I sprawled across the struggling dog and held his head tightly in my hands, being careful to keep away from Duke's snapping teeth. Bob began to pluck out the quills. Some came out easily but others had been driven in deep and held on stubbornly.

Bob held one up for me to see. "It's those barbs that hold them in," he explained. "They're just like tiny fish hooks."

Duke complained bitterly but Bob continued to pluck out the offending little lances. "There," he said finally. "Eighty-five! Only ones left are those three that broke off. I sure wish I had a pair of pliers."

"We could take them out after we get home," I suggested.

"Nope, they might work in out of sight by then," Bob replied. "Hold him really still now; I'm going to pull them out with my teeth."

"He was sitting on a low branch of a pine tree, seemingly at peace with the world."

And he did! Free of the painful quills at last, Duke bounded about us, whining and licking his face, eyes begging for sympathy.

"Okay boy," Bob said, patting Duke and avoiding a moist kiss Duke aimed at his face. "But next time use your head, huh? Nobody fools around with a porcupine!"

"Hey, let's go see if it's still around," I suggested.

"Sure," agreed Bob. "You stay behind us, Duke."

The warning was not needed. Duke wasn't having anything more to do with porcupines.

The porcupine wasn't hard to find. He was sitting on a low branch of a pine tree, eyes closed and seemingly at peace with the world. Probably he had already forgotten about the incident with the dog.

"That's a big fellow," Bob exclaimed. "He must weigh 25 or 30 pounds." His eyes ranged up the trunk of the tree. "Hey, looks like he's been feeding up there."

I followed Bob's glance and saw where the bark had been peeled from the pine trunk in several places. Porcupines love the tender bark of evergreen trees.

One day we found a small porcupine in a tree that stood at the edge of our garden. There was evidence that she had helped herself to carrots and lettuce and Mother was unhappy at the prospect of having her as a steady boarder.

I volunteered to climb the tree and bring her down. Before

starting up I prudently pulled on heavy leather work gloves. Prickly porky paid little attention to me as I climbed nearer. However, as I paused within reach, she suddenly thrashed her tail back and forth. As her quills were shaken loose, one of them rattled down the trunk and stuck into my exposed wrist. It's easy to guess how the myth started that porcupines shoot their quills at their enemies.

"Take it easy!" Bob called from the ground.

Carefully I reached around the tree trunk and caught hold of the nervous tail, drawing backwards with my gloved hand to smooth down the needle-sharp spears. Then, gripping the tree tightly with my knees, I put my other hand between her front legs and lifted her slowly from her perch. Well and good. I had caught her, but what should I do next? I would need one hand free to climb down from the tree.

In the end I allowed her to cling to my shoulder while I lowered myself down the trunk. I was careful to hold tightly to the dangerous tail. Porky showed no inclination to bite or claw.

When we had taken a close look at our woodland pincushion, we took her a mile away from the garden and released her with a peace offering of carrots. Quite undisturbed, she settled down to eat, then lazily climbed up to the crotch of another tree and promptly went to sleep.

Our next encounter with a porcupine was sometime later when Bob and I were spending a few days camping. One day we returned

to our camp to find that something had eaten a good part of our axe handle. It didn't take long to solve the mystery: a sleepy porcupine was tucked away in a nearby tree. We guessed that the axe handle had become salty from the grip of numerous sweaty hands and this had made it a delicacy for the salt-hungry marauder.

Porcupines (the name comes from two French words meaning spiny pig) are not difficult to find for they live in a wide range across North America, particularly in Canada and the northern States. In some areas they are protected by Wildlife Statute because they are so easy to capture, even without a gun or other weapon. Sometimes porcupines wander into grainfields and usually trample more grain than they eat, and occasionally they will anger a rancher when a too-curious cow or sheep gets a nose full of quills. Other than this, these inoffensive animals mind their own business and live in peace with their neighbours.

Of course, some woodland predators may think that the slow and peaceful porcupine would make an easy dinner. Almost without exception, they find out that porcupines are to be seen but not touched! Those who ignore the warning swish of a prickly tail have many painful days ahead to remind them of their folly.

As Bob and I learned more about the habits of the animals who shared our wilderness life, we were greatly impressed with the way Nature made sure that each had a defense against its enemies. The porcupine, prickly pincushion of the forest, is one of the most interesting examples.

A Curious Tail

BOB AND I HAD A MYSTERY. WE had a tail—a whole lot of tails—without an owner! We were anxious to find an answer to the puzzle, but even our dad couldn't help us.

When we left the ranchhouse to do morning chores, we often found the tail of a small animal lying on the steps. It was always the same: soft grey and tan in colour, about six inches long and an inch wide. There were no other clues, but Ginger the cat was usually nearby, a satisfied look on her face. It was puzzling to us that our cat should find this animal yet we never caught sight of it.

There were a lot of squirrels about, chattering from trees or playing games of tag with Ginger. They had long bushy tails but these were red and not nearly as soft as our puzzling find. There were rats with soft grey tails, but a rat's was narrow and round. There were chipmunks and ground squirrels. None of these tails matched the mysterious remains on the ranchhouse steps.

One day Bob and I went into the woods in search of firewood. We soon found what we were looking for, a tall dead pine whose branches were dead and whose trunk, battered by woodpeckers, was seamed and cracked—a good dry tree for wood. Our axes bit deep into the trunk.

"Timber!" Bob shouted as the tree began to sway. Just at that moment a small grey animal darted out of a hole in the trunk and scampered up the tree.

"He'll be killed!" I cried out, thinking that it was a red squirrel. There was no other tree near enough for the squirrel to jump to safety.

I was mistaken both in identification and in my estimate of how far this animal could jump. Just as the tree cracked and swayed toward the ground, the strange little animal launched itself into the air towards another tree at least thirty feet away.

"It will never make it!" Bob shouted.

Suddenly the furry stranger sprouted wings—at least that was what it looked like. Front and hind legs spread wide to reveal folds of skin that converted the small creature into a glider. It

"Suddenly the furry stranger sprouted wings..."

plunged downward, rapidly gaining speed, then soared upward, easily reaching the far-off tree. A grey furry tail formed a rudder to guide it in its flight.

While Bob and I watched in amazement, the small critter ran up the trunk of the new tree then launched into the air again, this time reaching a tree even farther away.

"Well, what do you know about that?" Bob exclaimed.

"It must be a flying squirrel!" I said excitedly. "I wonder why we've never seen one before?"

"Well, Ginger has," Bob replied. "Did you see that wide furry tail?" The mystery was solved!

That evening we opened an encyclopedia and found more answers. Flying squirrels are *nocturnal.* That means they come out at night to feed and are almost never seen in the daytime. That was the reason Ginger, hunting after dark, found the new breed of squirrel, and why we had never run across one before. We were pleased with our discovery of another neighbour.

Sometime later Bob and I were faced with a new mystery. In one of the ranch buildings we kept a wooden bin of grain to feed the stock. As winter approached we were puzzled to find chips of wood and small bundles of moss in the grain bin. It was several months before we found the answer to this riddle.

One night I was doing chores by lantern light. As I entered the storage shed to get a bucket of grain for the milk cow, I heard a rapid scurrying near the bin. Holding the lantern high, I was surprised to see a rat with a large wood chip in its mouth. Suddenly I guessed the mystery of the grain bin. This was a packrat, sometimes called a *trader* rat. With winter approaching, it was filling its own storehouse with grain but, true to the species, it never took grain without leaving something in exchange. This time it was a chip of wood.

I grinned. Well, I wouldn't expect a rat to know that grain was more valuable than wood chips! Ginger apparently did not like to dine on rats for we never found any sign that she caught one of the furry traders.

Bob and I had other interesting encounters with the small creatures who shared our wilderness. One winter when we were feeding cattle at meadows some distance from home, and staying in a log cabin, we found another small animal we had not seen before.

When our family first moved into the outpost cabin, we discovered that field mice had moved in ahead of us. Every night the uninvited guests raided the pantry and left their marks all through the food stores. Even traps didn't provide any lasting relief; as soon as one mouse was caught, another moved in.

One day we realized that the mice were gone—at least the raids on the food stores had stopped. Bob and I tried to figure out what had happened. What had driven the mice away? Then we found the answer, a very small answer indeed!

We were seated at the table one night when I saw a small creature scurry across the floor.

"Hey, there's a mouse!" I exclaimed and jumped up so suddenly my chair went over with a crash.

"Oh no, I thought they were all gone!" Mother's voice reflected her dismay. "Where did it go? Not in my flour bin, I hope."

"No way," Bob said, pointing. "Gary's chair must have come down on top of it!"

There on the floor beside the table was a small grey-tan creature lying on its back, not a movement to show that it was alive.

"Say, this isn't a mouse!" I said, looking more closely at the small, still creature. "What is it, Bob?"

"... I was surprised to see a rat with a large wood chip in its mouth."

"I think it's a shrew," Bob answered. "I've seen pictures of them."

We knelt down for a closer look and saw a long pointed nose over a mouth that bristled with sharp little teeth. The stump of a tail was smooth, almost hairless, quite unlike that of a mouse. I went to the encyclopedia for more information. The shrew, I learned, was a flesh-eater with a big appetite. It needed its full body weight in meat every day to survive. Mice were its favourite food. The mystery of the disappearing mice was solved.

That wasn't the end of our discovery about shrews. When we went to have another look at the small newcomer, it had disappeared. Another mystery! It didn't take long to solve this one. A few days later the shrew again ran across the kitchen floor. I stamped my foot and was surprised to see the shrew fall over on its side, kick its feet feebly, then lie still, apparently dead.

"Something strange about that!" I said. "I didn't hurt it at all. Let's watch for a bit."

A short time later the shrew stirred, looked about warily, then scampered under the woodbox. He was only pretending to be dead—until it was safe to scurry away!

We often saw the shrew after that, and he became quite tame. We named him Benny, and were glad to make him welcome in the kitchen in exchange for keeping the mice away.

Bob and I were always excited to see the larger animals—

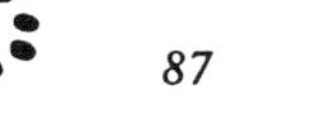

moose and deer and bear—but there were also interesting things to learn about the little creatures. We had more mysteries to solve as we became acquainted with the small neighbours who shared our wilderness. Living on a northern ranch was full of discovery and adventure.

Serenaders At Sunset

"GO EASY, BOB, WE DON'T WANT to spook those birds," I whispered, setting a foot down carefully to avoid a dry branch.

"Just crawl easy and *keep still,*" Bob hissed back. He led the way, taking advantage of a fallen tree to conceal our approach.

It was sunset of an early summer day. Bob and I had a hunch that a family of sandhill cranes had settled down for the night in a small swamp meadow, and we were anxious to see the big birds close up. Dick and Tony were tied to a tree well back in the woods, waiting while

we crept up to the swamp.

The fallen tree led us to the edge of brush that grew around the meadow and gave us the advantage of a ready made screen. We crouched below this tangle for a minute to allay suspicion in case anything out beyond had heard our careful approach; we then slowly raised our heads for a peek.

The cranes were there all right, but we were disappointed to find that they were on the far side of the meadow, too far to observe them well. Moreover, we noted that one old bird was acting as sentinel and was already looking in our direction. It would not be possible to get any closer to the flock.

I was about to stand up when Bob's hand tightened on my shoulder. Something had caught his attention nearer at hand. Then I saw it too, and froze. It looked like a puppy—no, two puppies, playing at the edge of the reeds twenty yards in front of us.

"Coyote pups!" Bob whispered excitedly.

"Think we could catch one?" I whispered back. What boy can resist the temptation to have a pup? We already had a moose calf at home.

"No way!" Bob whispered back. "Remember what Dad said? *Don't bother wild animals.* Besides, you can't tame a coyote."

We watched the antics of the two pups and decided that they were hunting rather than just playing. One leaped high in the air to knock down a dragon fly. The other pup nosed through a

"Only when the pups are small do they use a den ..."

clump of grass and flushed out a field mouse. He pounced and missed, then pounced again, eagerly snuffling under his paws. The mouse was more experienced in dodging coyotes than the pup was in hunting—it escaped and the disappointed pup turned away to join the other in catching grasshoppers.

Suddenly the stillness was shattered by a frightening noise close at hand:

Yip! Yip! Owoooooo!

Every hair on my neck was standing on end and my wildly beating heart told my feet to run!

Bob held up his hand to keep me silent and pointed to a knoll off to our left. At first I saw nothing, then the howl came again and led me to its source. A full-grown coyote, probably mother of the pups, stood on the hill, her head pointed to the sky while her throat vibrated with a mournful wail.

Although I had often heard the sunset serenade of coyotes, it had always been off in the distance. Close at hand and unexpected, it was a startling sound that froze us in our tracks. I moved slightly to get a better look and unwittingly snapped a branch. Instantly there was a warning bark, the pups scuttled to the hill and all three coyotes faded into the bushes.

Coyotes were some of the most familiar of the wild animals Bob and I came to know in our life on the cattle ranch. Midway in size between a fox and its larger cousin, the wolf, coyotes have shown a remarkable ability to co-exist with civilization. Their

range, from the Western Plains to the Pacific Coast, and from Mexico to Alaska, has not changed much since the first settlers arrived. While wolves and other larger animals shy away from people and their dwellings, coyotes seemed to look upon expanding civilization as a new source of food.

In spite of the fact that coyotes occasionally take sheep or lambs, or raid an exposed chicken flock, they have generally been useful neighbours to ranchers. Their principal sources of food are mice, rabbits and grasshoppers, all of which damage and destroy crops. Coyotes act as a natural check on these pests. Where coyotes have been destroyed by bounty hunters using traps and poisoned baits, there has been a rapid increase of rodents and accompanying headaches for farmers and ranchers.

Although coyotes are normally shy animals who run when approached, they are also very curious and sometimes quite bold. I remember how startled I was one day when I discovered a pair of coyotes slinking along behind me as I walked a woodland trail. When I stopped, they stopped, and when I moved on they followed at a respectful distance. I wondered at their boldness but when it happened on other occasions, I decided that it was just curiosity on the part of the coyotes. Certainly coyotes offer little threat to human beings, large or small.

It seemed to us that coyotes tried to play games with our dogs, Duke and Chuck. One coyote would start howling beyond the ranch buildings and the dogs would run barking in pursuit. A

minute later there would be another howl from the opposite direction, sending Duke and Chuck rushing back through the yard and across the meadow—only to hear the howl repeated from the first position. This would sometimes continue for an hour or more and I'm sure the two coyotes enjoyed the merry chase they gave our dogs.

Whenever our dogs spotted a coyote they would give immediate chase, but they were no match for the coyote's speed. On the other hand, coyotes—if there are two or three of them—are not above chasing a dog. One morning I stepped out the door of our ranchhouse just in time to see Duke and Chuck come

"A full-grown coyote stood on the hill, her head pointed to the sky ... "

racing through the gate with their tails between their legs. Startled, I looked out into the meadow in time to see three coyotes turn and trot away. Obviously they had teamed up to make our dogs run for their lives.

Coyotes live a nomadic life, ranging freely over a large territory. Only when the pups are small do they use a den, usually a hole dug deep under the roots of a fallen tree or else under a rocky outcropping. The pups are born in the dens in early spring and are well cared for by both coyote parents. By autumn they are full grown and ready to support themselves with the hunting skills taught by their parents.

The coyote's howl is its trademark and the West would never be the same without it. Almost every evening we could hear them howling in the distance, answering one another from hilltop to hilltop in a musical serenade to coming night. What did they have to say to one another? We often wondered. After much practice, Bob and I developed the ability to mimic them and it was always a thrill when we could get a coyote to howl back.

Many years have passed since Bob and I roamed the woods of the Cariboo. Where I live now I can hear the rumbling of diesel trains, and see shiny jetliners bridging continents with their long white trails. Yet it is a source of continuing pleasure that I can still see flocks of geese and sandhill cranes passing overhead in their migratory paths, and sometimes, of an evening in spring,

hear the sunset serenade of coyotes howling from a nearby ridge.

And sometimes on a summer night when the sky is filled with twinkling stars, my mind goes back to that night on our journey North when Bob and I first heard the coyote's mournful howl. On the brink of a new life we had thrilled to the promise of fun and adventure. And that promise had been fulfilled over and over again. The forests and waterways had shared their secrets with us and every day taught us something new. There would be many more adventures with our woodland neighbours in this friendly wilderness we called our home.

Will my grandchildren have the same thrill? It all depends on how good we are as stewards of Planet Earth. *Conservation* is a very important concept. What it means is that we should be good neighbours, not only with people around us, but also with birds and animals with whom we share our world. Will you do your part?